# BECAUSE I'M NEW

## Brad Sneed

PUBLISHED BY SLEEPING BEAR PRESS

They're home!

For Kristin — my oldest friend

♡

All inquiries should be addressed to: SLEEPING BEAR PRESS™ | 2395 South Huron Parkway, Suite 200 | Ann Arbor, MI 48104 | www.sleepingbearpress.com | © Sleeping Bear Press

Printed and bound in the United States. | 10 9 8 7 6 5 4 3 2 | Library of Congress Cataloging-in-Publication Data | Names: Sneed, Brad, author, illustrator.

Title: Because I'm new / Brad Sneed. | Other titles: Because I am new

Description: Ann Arbor, MI : Sleeping Bear Press, [2021] | Audience: Ages 4–8. | Summary: A new baby in the family means many changes—from late-night diaper changes to learning new ways to play—but here, baby tells their older sibling just what to expect. | Identifiers: LCCN 2020039829 | ISBN 9781534110717 (hardcover) | Subjects: CYAC: Babies—Fiction. | Brothers and sisters—Fiction.

Classification: LCC PZ7.S6713 Be 2021 | DDC [E]—dc23 | LC record available at https://lccn.loc.gov/2020039829

I am new.

You are big.

I've been waiting a
**long time**
to meet you.

Because I'm new,
there are things I cannot do.

catch.

But I can see.
I like to watch you play.

And I can hear.
I like the sound of your voice.

Because I'm new, mostly I'm quiet.

But sometimes I'm loud.

I cry when I'm hungry.

I cry when I'm uncomfortable.

Sometimes I cry and cry and CRY,
and no one knows why.

Because I'm new, I need lots of help.
Mom helps.

Dad helps.

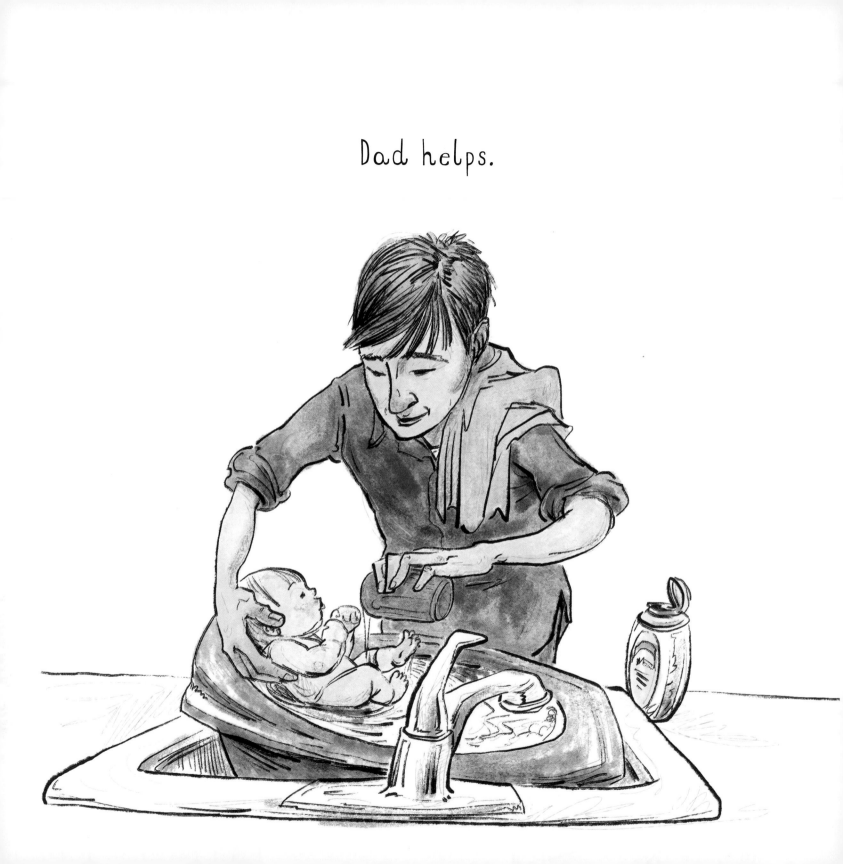

You can help, too!

Helping is hard.

Mom is tired.
Dad is tired.
You are tired, too.

Watch me grow . . .

and grow . . .

and grow.

I am still not big. But I am . . .

less new.

Because I'm less new,
there are new things
I can do.

catch.

1-2-3- Go!

But I still like to
watch you play.

And I still like the
sound of your voice.

I still cry.

But mostly,

I giggle.

And laugh.

And even though
I'm less new,
I will always
need your help.

my oldest friend!

And you will always be . . .